STEP BROTHER *with Benefits*

77

SECOND SEASON

Mia Clark

Copyright © 2015 Mia Clark

All rights reserved.

Stepbrother With Benefits 11 is a work of fiction. Names, characters, places, and incidents either are the product of the author's imagination or are used fictitiously. Any resemblance to actual persons, living or dead, events, or locales is entirely coincidental.

ISBN: 1517393728
ISBN-13: 978-1517393724

Book design by Cerys du Lys
Cover design by Cerys du Lys
Cover Image © Depositphotos | avgustino

Cherrylily.com

DEDICATION

Thank you to Ethan and Cerys for helping me with
this book and everything involved in the process.
This is a dream come true and I wouldn't have been
able to do it without them. Thank you, thank you!

CONTENTS

ACKNOWLEDGMENTS

Thank you for taking a chance on my book!

I know that the stepbrother theme can be a difficult one to deal with for a lot of people for a variety of reasons, and so I took that into consideration when I was writing this. While this is a story about forbidden love, it's also a story about two people becoming friends, too. Sometimes you need someone to push you in your life, even when you think everything is fine. Sometimes you need someone to be there, even when you don't know how to ask them to stay with you.

This is that kind of story. It is about two people becoming friends, and then becoming lovers. The forbidden aspects add tension, but it's more than that, too. Sometimes opposites attract in the best way possible. I hope you enjoy my books!

STEPBROTHER WITH BENEFITS

1 - Ethan

HEADING BACK TO OUR CAMPSITE is a disaster. I want to be calm and cool and relaxed, but I just can't. I really fucking can't stop getting pissed off at all of this shit that's been going on for, what, just a few days?

A few days is nothing in the grand scheme of life, the universe, and everything, but that doesn't change the fact that it's the first few days of me dating Ashley. If the first few days are so fucking difficult, what do you think the rest of it's going to be like?

Usually I'd just quit. It's not like I do this often, but if I know something isn't worth doing, then why should I bash my head against a wall trying to do it? Nah, there's just no fucking point, and so I'd cut it out and move on to something else.

If you think I'm going to quit being with Ashley, you're probably new around here. Like that Caleb kid. Who the hell does he think he is, anyways? I still don't know why the fuck he was wandering through the woods like that. I guess Ashley and I weren't exactly hiding all that well, but I didn't think we were being too noisy, either.

This whole situation just pisses me off, and while we walk back to the campsite to return to my dad and her mom, I get even more pissed off. It's not like I want to be pissed off, but apparently that's my default setting right now. What ever happened to being happy and carefree? Fuck if I know.

Our parents are there, and they're packing up some stuff, which confuses the fuck out of me at first. It's sandwiches, I guess. And a backpack. They've got the fishing poles out, too. I literally have no clue what's going on.

"Hey," my dad says, smiling at the two of us. "Everything alright?"

Nah, it's not. I don't say that, though. I just grunt.

"Yup!" Ashley says, lifting her chin. "Ethan helped me find the bathroom."

Oh, yeah. That's what we were supposed to be doing before, right? We did go there after, but my actual plan was to just drag her into the woods and have some fun with her. I don't think that ended up going so well, but at least we found the bathroom after.

"We were thinking about heading out," my stepmom says, smiling. "Why waste a perfectly good day just sitting around the campsite when we can enjoy the great outdoors!"

Yeah, well, that's a great idea and all, and I'd seriously enjoy it, too, except this issue with Caleb is still hanging over my head, and...

Wait. Wait a second here. Calm the fuck down, alright? If we all leave, which is exactly what the plan is, then Caleb won't find us when he heads over here in an hour. I have no clue why he wants to wait an hour to get this over with, but I guess it can work. It'll work for me, at least, and then it'll also work for Ashley.

I'm guessing Caleb will get bored. If he can't find us, then he'll end up forgetting about it. Or I can make up some excuse, tell him it was all in his head. Yeah, you know what, Caleb? You didn't see me with my hand shoved into Ashley's panties and my finger deep inside her. You didn't see me trying to coax an orgasm out of her delicious as fuck body, the heel of my hand pressed against her perfect fucking pussy. I don't know what you're talking about, bro. She's my sister! That's just real fucking disgusting.

Maybe he'll buy it. A guy can hope, right? If we're not here when he comes by, it gives me more time at least. Maybe I can figure this shit out and come up with an answer that doesn't completely screw me over.

Yeah, that's it.

2 - Ashley

So," MY MOM SAYS while we're walking through the woods. "What do you two think about splitting up and having a little mother-daughter and father-son bonding time this afternoon?"

I'm carrying two of the fishing poles and my mom has one of the empty cooler cases we brought, along with the worms Ethan and his dad got earlier, plus a few other things. Ethan's carrying the backpack slung over his back and his dad has our food and a picnic blanket. I'm not entirely sure what we're doing, except it involves walking through the woods and also fishing.

"What's that supposed to mean?" Ethan asks.

We've been walking in the woods for awhile now. We climb up over a small ridge and the woods vanish ahead of us, replaced by a rocky hill, and beyond that an open lake. It's hidden away in the woods, and it's not exactly huge, but it looks like it would take awhile to swim across it.

"We were going to come here alone before, remember?" Ethan's dad says to him. "I thought it'd be nice if we just had some alone time and gave the ladies their time, too. We can meet back up for dinner."

Ethan gives his dad a weird look. I'm not sure what exactly it's for, but he doesn't look too thrilled about the idea of splitting up.

"We can go fishing, Ashley," my mom says to me. "We'll see if we can catch something nice for dinner."

"Mhm, and we'll take a hike through the woods," Ethan's dad says to him. "There's a trail by the river that feeds into the lake and I thought it'd be nice to check it out."

It looks like everything's been decided and it's just up to us to agree, but...

I don't really know if I want to? It's not that I don't want to, and I'd love to spend some time with my mom, but, um... what about Ethan? I know he's stressed right now, because how could he not be? I'm stressed, too, but I just have this strange feeling that everything is going to be fine. Maybe I'm being intentionally obtuse and delusional right now, but I just want everything to work out.

Isn't this kind of like what happened with Jake, though? I thought I could be with him before, and in reality he was just using me. Then, after that, when he found out I was sleeping with my step-brother after I accidentally sent him those incriminating text messages, well...

I know it sounds stupid, because I'm supposed to be smart. I *am* smart, at least as far as book smarts are concerned, but there's so many other ways to be smart, and I'm just not sure how all of them work. Street smarts, or social awareness, or intuition and instinct.

I've watched Ethan be Ethan for years now. I've seen him flawlessly interact with all sorts of people, and sometimes I've wondered how he does it so easily. It's not like that's something you can just watch and copy, you know? There's more to it than that, but I don't know what exactly that is or what it means.

I've seen him play football and move so athletically, and even though I could probably explain to you exactly how he's moving, I couldn't move that way on my own. Sometimes it's the small, simple things that are the hardest. If you can do something so extremely complicated, but make it seem incredibly easy... that's what being smart is.

I suppose that's how I am with book smarts, though. I understand intellect and problem-solving like it's my second nature, but that comes harder for other people.

We all have our strengths and weaknesses. We're all good at something and bad at something else. This is why we need each other. This is why it makes sense for Ethan and I to be together.

I'm the good girl, the careful, cautious one, who thinks before she acts. Ethan is the bad boy, the risk taker, the person who jumps into action regardless of the consequences. Sometimes you can't wait to think before you act, though. Sometimes you can't be careful or cautious. And sometimes you need to know when a risk is too great, and when you should reign in your recklessness and consider the repercussions.

This is why we're perfect together. I'm sure there's a lot more reasons, but I think that's one of them.

I *see* Ethan, too. I really see him, I understand him. I think he understands me, as well. He's not just a bad boy, at least not to me. He's careful with me, he's patient and kind with me. He's understanding, also. Ethan isn't reckless with me and he doesn't take careless risks with me.

When I'm with Ethan, I feel a little risky, though. I want to try more. I want to be a little reckless and more carefree. I feel like I can let my guard down, because I trust him not to hurt me.

I love him so much...

Ethan's voice snaps me out of my thoughts and reverie.

"I need to talk to Ashley about it," he says. "Alone."

This is... what?

"Huh?" I say.

"Um..." Ethan's dad looks confused.

"Listen," Ethan says. "You two decided on this while we were gone. I get it, alright? I really do, and I understand that it's a cool idea, but you decided it without us, didn't even ask us. So, yeah, I want to talk to Ashley about it. Alone. And we'll decide what we want to do. I think that's fair, don't you? It's the same thing you two were doing."

"Ethan, it's not like we're making earth-shattering plans here," his dad says. "I didn't think it was that important."

"It's important to me," Ethan says, refusing to budge.

My stepdad looks upset, and I can understand why. He's not used to this. He's the boss most of the time, in business and otherwise, and he's used to people listening to what he has to say. He's open to discussing any issues that arise, but he's not exactly confronted with outright insubordination most of the time.

That's exactly what Ethan is, though. He's insubordination incarnate. His dad might have forgotten that, but Ethan's been the bad boy who refuses to listen to anyone but himself for a long time.

He listens to me, though. He basically just told that to his dad, too. I don't want them to fight, but it makes me smile that Ethan wants to stand up for me like that.

"Oh, let's just let them talk," my mom says, laughing. "We did kind of decide on all of this without them, so Ethan isn't wrong. We should have waited so we could talk it over together."

The only thing is that if we'd waited too long, Caleb would have shown up. What would have happened then?

"Alright. That's fine," my stepdad says, though he doesn't look like it's fine. "We'll go to the lake. You two talk and figure out what you want to do, then come find us."

"Don't get lost in the woods!" my mom says, grinning.

My stepdad rolls his eyes at her and laughs. It's going to be pretty hard to get lost in the woods considering the lake is clearly visible from here and I doubt Ethan and I are going too far. Our parents head to the lake to set up everything for fishing. Ethan grabs my hand and drags me a little further into the woods. We head off the beaten path and further into privacy. I'm not sure if this is a good idea or not, but...

As soon as we're alone and isolated, Ethan is on me. He pins me to a tree and frantically grabs at the button of my shorts. He has it undone, my shorts unzipped, pulling them down to my ankles before I can say anything or protest. As soon as I gather my wits and start to open my mouth to talk, he's kissing me.

"Just shut the fuck up, Princess," he says, smirking at me. "I don't want to talk right now."

"I thought this was supposed to be about talking!" I say, laughing.

"Yeah, well, I changed my mind. I just want to be inside you."

The way he says it, with honesty and lust, it surprises me. It's sexy, but it's also real and raw. I can feel his intensity, his eyes staring into mine. He fumbles with his own shorts, letting them fall to the ground, then he pulls his underwear down enough to reveal his erect, throbbing cock. I glance down and stare at it for a second, but I don't have time for much more.

Effortlessly, Ethan grabs my thighs and lifts me up. My back slides against the bark of the tree behind me, and I squeak a little in protest. I don't manage to do much else before he has my panties pulled aside and his cock pushed inside of me. He fills me completely, pressing deep into me, and I let out a gasp and a moan. We're pressed so tight together right now that we might as well be one person instead of two.

I wrap my legs around him as he pulls out a little and thrusts back in. This is fast, but it's also steady. I hear Ethan grunting in my ear, his body pounding against mine. Thankfully I'm still mostly clothed, but I can feel the scrape of the tree bark grinding against my shirt and my back. It doesn't hurt, it's just rough. I like when Ethan's rough with me, but this is something else entirely.

"You're inside me," I say, whispering to him. "Is this what you wanted?"

"Fuck yes," he says, his teeth latching onto my neck. "You have no fucking clue what you do to me, Princess. I can't even fucking think sometimes. The only thing I can think about is you, about fucking you and thrusting my cock deep inside you."

"How much?" I ask him. "How much do you want me?"

Ethan thrusts hard into me and practically growls in my ear. "I want every fucking inch of you, Ashley," he says. "Inside and out, all of you. I want your body and your soul, your mind and your heart, I just... I fucking want *you*. I want you to want me, too. I love you, Princess, I..."

It's just... it's so strange to hear him talk like that. I'm not sure what to do or say, because I'm not sure I've ever heard Ethan say anything even remotely similar to what he just said. It's so honest and genuine, like he's opening up to me, but that's what he's been doing for awhile now, isn't it?

I know this, and I realized it long before now, but his words right now, right in the heat of his passion, they do something to me. They make me feel even more than I've already felt, but I'm not even sure what these feelings are. Love, yes, and lust, and need. I feel a greedy lust, an inherent desire, and as much as he wants to be inside me, I want him inside me, too.

I feel like we counter each other, but we also complement each other. We're opposites in a lot of ways, but sometimes opposites attract, and...

They attract hard. Really really hard. So fucking hard...

I'm lost and gone but I'm here in the moment, too. I'm close and closed off and the only thing I can feel or think about is us. I don't know where we are, but it doesn't even matter. We're here, together. I feel the warmth and strength of Ethan's body tight against mine. I can feel the tightness of the muscles in his core grinding against my clit and the throbbing strength of his erection pressing hard into me. He fills me, but it's more than that, too.

He fills a part of me that I never knew needed to be filled before. I give him something that he never knew he was missing.

I clench my eyes shut and let myself feel everything. It's so much, so rough, so intense. Ethan thrusts hard into me one final time, ready to unleash inside of me. That's all I need, and I give in to his carnal demands. My body shudders in ecstasy, quivering and shaking, trapped between him and the tree behind me, with my legs wrapped around his body and my fingers tangled in his hair.

He grinds his hips against me, his cum crashing inside me.

I'm his. And he's mine. We're together.

I want to collapse in a heap on the ground but instead Ethan pulls me close and holds me in his arms. I'm part cradled, part clinging to him, fully loving him, and he hugs me tight. He's still inside me, but there's no frantic, frenzied rush anymore.

That's when I fully realize what exactly we just did.

"Um..." I say to him, smiling, sheepish. "Our parents are right over there."

I don't know where over there is, but I'm pretty sure it's only a few minutes walk.

"Yeah, so?" he answers, grinning at me. "You think I care?"

"I think you should!" I say, laughing. "What if they see us like this?"

"Yeah, well, alright, uh..." He's quiet for a second, thinking. "Look, I think we should do what they planned. I'll go with my dad and you hang out with your mom. Just for the afternoon, alright?"

"Sure," I say, giving him a funny look. "That's not why you wanted to talk to me alone, is it? Or, um... was..."

Sex? I mean, that's a pretty good reason to be alone, but I'm not sure that's what he planned, either.

"Nah, that's not it," Ethan says, smirking at me. "Pretty fucking amazing, though, right? You're always pretty fucking amazing, Princess."

I laugh and blush, burying my head in the crook between his neck and his shoulder. "Shush, you," I say.

We're quiet for a moment, just holding each other, reveling in the afterglow of our mutual orgasm.

"I'm going to tell him," Ethan says after awhile. "That's what I wanted to talk to you about. I'll go with my dad and I'm going to tell him about us. I don't know exactly when. I'll figure it out. It's going to be really fucking hard for me, Princess. I'm going to do it, though. I just wanted you to know, that's all. When we come back, he'll know, and then everything will be fine."

I'm not sure if that's true. I understand what he means, and I know that he's probably doing this because of Caleb catching us in the woods earlier, but what about the rest? Everything might be fine in regards to Caleb, but it might be really bad as far as Ethan's dad is concerned.

"Everything *will* be fine," I tell him, kissing his cheek softly. "I know your dad will understand."

"Yeah... I sure hope so."

We kiss, really kiss. This isn't a kiss for any specific reason, it's just a kiss because we love each other. I know he loves me and he knows I love him, and it's as simple as that.

At least it's as simple as that for now. I'm not sure if it's going to stay that way, or for how long, but whatever happens, I know we can push through it.

3 - Ethan

HOLY FUCK. SERIOUSLY, FUCK. Fucking, fucking...
fuck.

I've done a lot of stupid shit before. I can own
it and accept it. I mean, yeah, sometimes it seemed
like a good idea at the time, but maybe in a good
bad idea kind of way, right? It's not a good thing to
do, but you do it thinking you won't get caught.
What's the worst that can happen?

This is not even close to that. This is just a
really good idea, but I don't want to do it at all. I
think that makes it a bad good idea. It's one of
those things that you know is the right thing to do,
but you just really don't want to do it. Yeah, well,
that's life, isn't it? What the fuck do I know?

My dad and I eat a quick lunch with Ashley and her mom. Nothing crazy here, just sandwiches and chips. It's nice hanging out by the lake. Not a lot of people come this way. They go to the river more, but even then it's a lot further up, by where the rocks have been shaped into natural slides and there's little pools you can hang out in. That's where the jumping spot is, too. Honestly, it's pretty fucking awesome there. You can jump off this thirty foot cliff into a pool of deep water, and it's just a huge rush.

I kind of feel like I'd rather jump off a three hundred foot cliff into a shallow pool of water than tell my dad about how I'm dating Ashley now, but whatever. There's no cliffs that high around here that I know of, and telling my dad is just something I have to do. I'll figure this shit out.

I hope we go for a long hike. A really really fucking long hike. I'm going to need some time here. I don't know how long. I'll figure it out as I go. That's mostly how I do everything, but usually it seems easier than this.

"You boys have fun, alright?" my stepmom says to me and my dad after we're done eating.

"Don't get into too much trouble!" Ashley says, winking at us.

My dad flexes, putting on a show of outdoor manliness or something. I just nod and smile and try to act normal, but I'm pretty sure it doesn't work. No one says anything, though. Ashley smiles at me.

Maybe I'll just go over right now and kiss her. Fucking... pull her in my arms and grab her ass, lift her up, and kiss her hard. That's a good way to tell my dad, right? If he doesn't get it after that, I don't know what to say. Actions speak louder than words or something. I'm pretty sure this is how that works.

Yeah, well, we're both bad with that. We don't really talk, and our actions have always spoken volumes, except none of it's been very good. Yeah yeah, my dad and I get along well enough, but I wouldn't exactly say we're close.

We have an understanding. I think that's how he'd explain it if this was business-speak. This isn't a "You Scratch My Back and I Scratch Yours" type of understanding, but a "You Leave Me Alone and I'll Do the Same For You" kind of one. In a friendly as fuck way, though. Companionable silence or some shit, just staying out of each other's hair.

I don't want to get into this right now, but I just don't want to deal with my dad or our current situation, so here you go. When my mom died, my dad tried to make it work, but he just couldn't. He couldn't really deal with it, and I didn't know what was going on, so he left. I wouldn't say he abandoned me, because he was always technically *there*, but I couldn't talk to him, couldn't do much with him.

We lived in the same fucking house, but we might as well have been worlds apart. This lasted for awhile. We'd go do stuff, go out to dinner sometimes, but neither of us was really there. I didn't know how to be there. I was just some little kid, didn't even know what was going on, except people kept telling me my mom was gone and she wouldn't be coming back.

How the fuck do you deal with that? I don't know. I still don't really know, but it's a decade in the past and I guess I've just gotten used to it. It's not like I'm ever going to forget, but sometimes it's hard to remember, too.

I remember my mom used to pack a swirly straw for my juice box back in elementary school. It wasn't anything crazy, just some goofy as fuck straw, but I liked it. It was different, and none of the other kids at school had one, so I felt cool. You know how kids are, when you get some new toy or whatever and you just feel like a badass? Yeah, that was me.

The first time I went back to school after my mom died and my dad made me my lunch, he forgot the straw. Actually, I don't even think he knew the straw existed. And then it's like... holy fuck, are you serious? I'm never going to see my mom again, and now you forget my straw?

It's not even important. I guess it was never about the straw. I don't know. I really loved that straw and it sounds stupid as fuck, but there you go. I went home and I was angry and my dad just kind of looked at me like he didn't know what to do. I marched into the kitchen, ripped open the cabinet where my mom kept the swirly straws, then I grabbed them all in my fist and stomped over to the trash.

I threw them away in front of him. He just looked at me, listless and slightly confused.

I know he didn't know what the straws meant to me. If I'm being real fucking honest, I'm not even sure if I know what the straws meant to me. They're just straws, you know?

That's me and my dad in a nutshell, though. I've learned that he doesn't understand me, and I've realized I don't understand him. It's easier that way. We can work with that, and we can get along. It doesn't need to be anything more than that.

Yeah, he's still my dad. I love him, because I'm supposed to love him. I actually do love him, too, but it's just... I don't think we'll ever really *know* each other. We'll never be as close as Ashley and her mom are.

I'm not sure if that's a bad thing. I don't know if it's *anything*, to be honest. It's just the way it is.

I realize we've been walking in the woods for awhile now without talking. I'm not sure where we're going. We went along the shore to the river at first, then crossed it by jumping over some rocks further up, and now we're heading into the great unknown.

There's a path, so it's not exactly completely unknown, but neither of us has been here for awhile.

"Hey," my dad says. "What do you say we take a detour?"

I give him a weird look and grin. "Yeah?"

"Yeah," he says, smiling. "Let's just go this way." He points to the right. "It should be fine. We'll be alongside the lake, and it shouldn't be hard to find our way back. It's different, though. A change of pace and something new."

That sounds good. I like it. A change of pace? Fuck, that's exactly what I need.

That's what I have with Ashley, and I think it'd be nice to have something like that with my dad, too.

Just something different. Something new.

"If we get lost, I'm blaming you," I tell him, smirking.

"Yeah yeah," my dad says, rolling his eyes. "I can accept that."

I want to ask him if he can accept me, though. Can he accept me and Ashley? Can he accept us dating?

I don't ask him that. We step off the dirt trail we were on and go to the right, hiking into the woods. There's no paths here, nothing to guide us, nothing to stop us.

This is my element. I don't follow the rules, I make my own. My dad's the same way, whether he wants to admit it or not. You don't become filthy fucking rich by playing it safe, now do you?

I guess that's a connection we have. We're not so different. I hope he agrees and I hope he understands me.

4 - Ashley

S O..." MY MOM SAYS TO ME, staring at the hook on the end of her fishing pole.

I smile, but I try not to laugh. "So..."

"I don't think we thought this over very well, Ashley."

"Mom, it's just a worm," I say.

"If Ethan and his father were here, we could have them do it. That's all I'm saying."

"It can't be that hard, can it?" I ask.

"Um... have you ever gone fishing before?" she asks. "Because I haven't."

"Not really, but..." Really, it can't be that hard, right?

I pull off the top of the little bucket of worms that Ethan and my stepdad bought at the store earlier, then ready the hook of my fishing pole. You just, um... you put the worm on the hook, right? I don't think there's much to it.

Closing my eyes, I reach into the dirt in the bucket until I find a worm. It's gross. And dirty. Well, duh! Of course it's dirty, Ashley! It's literally in a bucket of dirt. It's fine, it's fine, it's...

I hurry and pull the worm out, then open my eyes. Don't look. Don't look at the worm in your fingers. I drape the worm over the hook and it just kind of hangs there, unassuming.

"I don't think that's how it works," my mom says.

"It's on the hook," I point out to her. It really is!

"Yes, but what happens when you put it in the water? It's not just going to stay on the hook, is it?"

"Oh, um..."

"Ashley, we're hopeless," my mom says. "Do you just want to go swimming instead?"

"We can't quit!" I tell her. "Mom, this is serious. We're supposed to be fishing. Also, we don't even have bathing suits."

She shrugs. "So? You're wearing underwear, aren't you? It's not like anyone else is here. It's practically the same thing."

I stare at her. "What? Are you being serious?"

"What do you mean? Of course I am. It's not like I haven't seen you in your underwear before. You were traipsing around upstairs just running out of Ethan's room in your bra and panties the other day, so don't even try to act like you don't have a wild streak. It's only swimming, too."

"Mom, someone else could come. I'm not going swimming in my underwear."

"Fine! Then we have to figure out how to go fishing," she says.

"I really don't think this is an either-or kind of situation. We can, um..."

I look around, trying to figure out what else we can do. Honestly, I have no idea. There's a lake, and that's about it. We can go back to the campsite, but it's not like that's a whole lot better.

"What if you tie it around the hook?" my mom offers.

"Like a knot? Tie the worm in a knot?"

"Yes, exactly."

"Um..." I stare at the worm. It does look long enough for me to tie it in a knot around the hook, so...

I give it a try, and it's just horrible. First off, shortly after she said that, the worm wriggled off the hook and fell to the ground. Second, as soon as I pick it back up, it starts squirming, and it doesn't ever stop squirming. Worms squirm. A lot. Ugh.

I manage to tie it in a knot around the hook, but then the worm starts to squirm and wriggle and untie itself. What the heck, worm?

"What if we just throw the hook in the water and pretend to fish?" I ask my mom. "That's really the important part, right? Even if you don't catch anything, fishing is supposed to be relaxing, so..."

"Oh! Oh, that's a good idea. I knew I could count on you," my mom says.

I quickly dump the worm back in its bucket and close the lid. My mom and I head to the edge of the lake and prepare to pretend to fish. We... um... so... the hooks are in the water, sort of. They do not go very far. We really didn't think this through all that well. They're in, though! We're fishing. Does it matter how far away the hooks are if we don't even have bait? I don't think so, but I really don't know, because I'm not sure what the rules are for pretend fishing.

We sit down next to the lake and bask in the glow of our fishing prowess. The water washes up the shore, lapping across the rocky sand.

"Is everything alright?" my mom asks me suddenly.

"Um, what do you mean?" I counter.

"With you and Ethan?" my mom says. "Have you two been able to talk at all?"

"Sort of?" I say. I don't know how to explain this. "We talked in the car on the ride here, and um... last night in the tent. We talked a little this morning, too. I guess it is hard. There's not a lot of privacy here."

"I know," my mom says. "It's supposed to be fun, but if you aren't having fun you can tell me, you know?"

"It's not that it's not fun, but..."

I don't know. I'm not sure what to tell her. I would tell her if I could, but I just don't know what to say.

"I can pretend to be sick if you want," my mom says. "Then we can go back home early."

'   "Mom..."

"I'm just saying," she says.

"I know, and I appreciate it, but..." I hesitate, not sure if I should tell her this, except why not? "Ethan is going to tell his dad," I say.

"When?" she asks.

"Now? Um... I don't know exactly when, but he said he would tell him while they're hiking, so probably he'll know by the time they come back."

"Oh my," my mom says. The way she says it makes me nervous.

"What's that supposed to mean?"

"What? Oh, nothing."

"Mom, seriously, what's wrong?"

"Nothing's wrong. I'm just wondering how this is going to go."

"What do you mean you're wondering how this is going to go? It's going to go fine!" I think it is. I really hope so. "...Right?"

"I'm sure it'll be fine," she says. "I was talking with Ethan's father last night and it wasn't anything too serious, but he did mention how he thinks Ethan is lashing out a little more lately and maybe he needs to have a talk with him about that. I tried to say it was probably nothing and Ethan's an adult now, but you know how his father can be."

"Um... and you didn't think you should tell us this?"

"If Ethan is lashing out, it's because of you, honey, so really, I think everything is going to be fine if him and his father talk."

"I guess..." I say. For a second I'm not sure what else to say, so I stay silent. "Mom, do they hate each other? I know they talk, but I don't know if they like each other."

"Of course they don't hate each other, Ashley. It's just complicated, that's all. They're men. You know how it is?"

I don't know how it is, actually, but I decide not to say anything.

"We need to help them," I tell her. "Whatever happens when they come back, we need to help them. If Ethan's dad is mad, then we need to all talk until they aren't mad anymore. I know that Ethan and his dad don't really talk much, but I don't care. They can't be mad at each other, not about this. It's going to be too hard if they get upset about it and get angry with each other."

My mom grins, an excited glimmer in her eyes. "What do you have in mind?"

"Um... I don't know. I didn't think that far ahead."

"Campfire cuddling," my mom says. "And storytelling. We can all talk about what we've been up to for the past year. I know you and I talk on the phone all the time, so we probably already know what we've been doing, but Ethan doesn't talk to his father much, so it'll be a chance for them to open up. But also we'll be seeing each other in a new light, and if I'm cuddling with your stepfather at one side of the campfire and you're cuddling with Ethan at the other, we can all look into each other's eyes and really see what's going on. What do you think?"

"I think it's a nice idea," I say. "I like it. If they don't want to talk about what they've been up to, we could tell stories, too. Ghost stories, maybe?"

"With s'mores, of course," my mom says, extremely serious, nodding.

"Of course!" I tell her, laughing.

"I think it'll work," she says, nodding again. "Like a double date, I guess, but also acknowledging each other. I acknowledge you, Ashley! Ethan, too."

I laugh at the way she says it. "Thanks?"

"So what else have you been up to?" she says. "When you and Ethan came back from the bathroom, you two looked a little strange. Did something happen?"

"Oh, um..."

Before I can say anything, someone comes up behind us. "Uh... Ashley?"

Oh my God, it's Caleb. Why is he here?

"Um... hi, Caleb?" I say, offering him a small wave.

"I saw a note at your campsite when I came to find you and it said you'd be here, so..."

"Hi, Caleb!" my mom says, waving excitedly at him.

"Hi," he says, sort of smiling and looking anxious at the same time.

"Here," my mom says. "Come sit with us. We're fishing."

"We're not actually fishing," I say, mumbling. "We didn't know how to put the worms on our hooks."

"Do you want me to show you?" Caleb asks, eager. "It's not that hard. Here, uh, where are your worms?"

My mom points to the bucket of worms behind us, just sitting there on the ground. Caleb goes to get it, then joins us.

This is weird. And awkward. I'm not sure what I'm going to say to Caleb. I guess it's not so bad since it's just me and my mom here? She already knows, so...

"Ashley, I don't mean to, uh... in front of your mom... but..."

"What?" my mom asks, concerned. "Is something wrong, you two?"

"Um..." I say, unsure what else to say.

"Er... well..." Caleb pauses after that.

I think that's going to be it and he won't say anything, but... nope...

5 - Ethan

I have no fucking clue where we are, and I'm pretty sure my dad doesn't, either. Neither of us is willing to admit this, though. I mean, fuck, maybe he does know? He had a good point before, too. Just because I don't recognize a damn thing around us, doesn't mean we're lost or anything. The lake should be to the right, so if we just turn that way, we'll be fine.

Just ignore the fact that we don't have a compass or anything. Also the fact that we haven't exactly been going in a straight line this entire time. How the fuck do you walk in a straight line in the middle of the woods? I guess you can try, but good luck with that.

We can probably just turn around, though. We know where we came from, so it's not like we can't just go back that way. Yeah, that's it. We're fine. It's cool...

"So tell me about this girl you're dating," my dad says, kind of serious but friendly.

"Yeah, she's cool," I say. That's it. Not sure I want to say more yet. Better not to incriminate myself when I finally tell him the truth.

"Who is she?" he says. "Do I know her?"

Shit. "Uh, maybe?"

"It's not one of Ashley's friends, is it?" my dad asks.

How the fuck do I even have this conversation? Someone help me out here, please, because I have no clue what I'm doing right now.

"Kind of?" I say. Ashley's probably friends with herself, right? Sure, let's go with that. "It's complicated."

"How long have you been dating her?" my dad asks. "Does she have a name? Give me something to work with here, Ethan."

He laughs, and I guess it is kind of funny. I'm being vague as fuck, but there's a damn good reason for it. I guess I could just come out and tell him right now, but I'm still not sure how to do it. You can say it's as easy as just saying it, but for me it's not that easy. I'm fine with doing everything else, but this shit is hard for me.

"Just uh... alright, well, you're going to think this is stupid, but we had a kind of friends with benefits situation at first, right?" Yeah, this is true.

Mostly true. Stepbrother with benefits, but whatever. "Yeah, so, it kind of escalated and now we're dating. It's only been, uh... not that long. A little more than a week, but I really like this girl."

My dad laughs. "Fair enough. I'm glad. Really, I know what you're probably thinking, but I'm glad you're finally taking a step in the right direction. I know I don't say this much, but I really am proud of you, Ethan. You've grown a lot. We've had some tough times, but..."

Yeah, that's it. My dad and I don't really talk, and when we do talk, it's a lot of trailing off and sort of implying shit, but we don't ever say it. We don't know how to say it.

We've had some tough times, but honestly we're just two really shitty people who fuck things up constantly and who the fuck knows how we found people who stay with us? I don't even know if Ashley's going to stay with me, but I don't want to fuck it up this time. My dad's found a good thing with Ashley's mom, but he's pissed off more than his fair share of people, too. Not in dating, but in other aspects of his life.

Yeah, well...

"Do you remember the first time we came here?" I ask him.

He gives me a weird look, then nods. "Yeah, I do."

"That was bad, huh?"

He doesn't say anything, just waits and listens.

"I know we don't talk about this kind of thing much, but I still know it was bad. I guess we got over it a little, but I was so angry with you, and I think you were angry with me. I--"

"Ethan, we don't have to talk about this," he says, kind of curt, not mean or rude, but I can tell he doesn't want to talk about it.

"Yeah, I know we don't, but I want to," I tell him.

"I'm not exactly proud of what happened back then," he says. "When your mother passed away, I just... I had a hard time coping. I loved her so much, Ethan. I love your stepmom, too, but it's different. I don't want you to think that I'm replacing your mother with Ashley's mom or anything like that."

"Listen," I say. "Stop. I don't think that. I just want to talk about this, alright?"

I don't know why. It's weird, because I don't think I actually want to talk about this. It's a hard conversation to have, but it's kind of like I'm procrastinating and if I have this hard conversation, it'll be easier than having the even harder conversation about me dating Ashley. I know I still have to have that one, but I feel like if I can just have this one first, then the other will be easier, and maybe it'll work out better?

I'm pretty sure this is the most fucked up idea I've ever had, but I'm not exactly known for my good ideas.

"I really like Ashley's mom. I like Ashley a lot, too. I'm not good at this emotional heartfelt conversation shit or whatever. I just want to tell you that I was really hurt back then, and I get why you were hurt, too, but I feel like maybe it would have been easier if we could have just been hurt together instead of apart."

"I know," my dad says, which surprises me. "I've thought about it a lot. I wasn't really there for you. I tried sometimes, and I tried to pull myself out of it, but every single time I looked at you, I remembered her. I still do, you know? Sometimes I close my eyes, and when I open them I see you and her again, almost as if no time has passed at all and we're all back together. It's like the last ten years of my life were a dream, and I've finally woken up. I can see her pushing you on the swings, and you laughing and yelling for her to push you faster and higher. I remember her telling you not to jump off the swing, but you always did. She'd rush over and yell you, but you'd both be laughing."

Fuck, man... this is rough. I think this is the longest my dad and I have talked about something like this in, uh... forever?

"I know it's stupid, but I always felt kind of left out," my dad says. "I felt like it was you and your mother, and me and your mother, but I was never a part of your life and even when the three of us were together, it was almost like we were only all together because of her. When she died, I didn't know what to do, Ethan. I wasn't sure how to be there for you, because I thought you needed her more than you needed me, and I needed her, too. I..."

"I need you," I tell him. It hurts to say it, but it's true. And fuck you, I'm not even fucking crying here. I've got something in my eye. Shut the fuck up. It's the woods and I've got allergies or whatever. Just fuck off.

My dad looks at me and he smiles and he's got allergies or something, too. Damn fucking woods. Should have brought some allergy medication. Holy fuck, this pollen is bad.

"I was really pissed off when you didn't pack the swirly straws in my lunch," I tell him, trying not to laugh. It sounds so dumb, but I really was so fucking pissed.

"I remember you threw them away," he says. "You know, I thought about putting one in your lunchbox that day? I didn't know if you'd like it, though. That was always a thing you and your mother shared. I guess that sounds dumb, but it used to make me smile when you and her played with those straws. I liked watching you blow bubbles with them in your milk and she'd get a straw and blow bubbles, too. You two always used to have so much fun together."

I don't know what the fuck to say to that. I wish he'd put a straw in with my lunch, but I'm not going to blame him for not doing it. I blamed him then, and I was seriously super fucking pissed, but it's like... uh, that was a long time ago. I don't even use straws anymore.

"I still have them," my dad says. "The straws. That's stupid, isn't it? I pulled them out of the trash when you weren't looking. I washed them and kept them hidden in my room. Sometimes I'd pour a glass of milk and bring it to my bedroom and lock the door, then use the straws, just to try and remember. It was never really the same, but it made me smile for a little while."

"We can blow bubbles in milk if you want," I say. Wow. Seriously? How fucking dumb can I get? I don't even know.

My dad laughs. "I think maybe we're both a little too old for that now, but I'd be willing to give it a try."

I smile and try to think, because I want to say something, but I'm not entirely sure how to say it.

"It was never between you and her," I say. "I never thought of you as separate from Mom. Yeah, you usually stood off to the side or whatever, but you were still there. I guess I always thought it was you keeping watch over us and protecting us. That's why I felt safe jumping off of the swings, Dad. It's not like I was going to die or anything, but when I jumped, I saw you down there, waiting, and I knew that when I hit the ground, you'd still be there. You were always there for us, and then..."

I don't know. I thought he was always there for me. This is something I've never talked about with anyone before.

I used to think my dad was there for me and Mom, but then when she died he wasn't there for me. He just kind of left, hid away, stopped paying attention to me, stopped... caring, I guess? I know he didn't, or at least I know that now, but that's how I felt then.

So then what if all the times I thought he was there for the both of us, he was only actually there for Mom? That's what my little kid self thought. What if he was never there for me to begin with? He wasn't there for me after she died, so...

"Ethan," my dad says, choking up. We're not walking anymore. We're standing by a tree, just kind of chilling, I guess. If you can even call it that. "That's... that's not what I meant to do. Is that what you thought? That..."

We can't keep doing this. We've just got to fucking own it, commit to it, and finally say the fucking words we want to say.

"Yeah," I tell him, and it's so fucking hard it hurts and I just want to fall on the ground and curl up in a ball, but I say it anyways. "When you stopped being there for me after mom died, I thought you were never there for me to begin with. I thought you were only there because of her, and now that she was gone, you didn't care anymore."

He just kind of stares at me. Huge fucking allergy issue right now, seriously. We're not two grown men crying in the middle of the fucking woods. How fucked up would that be?

I guess we've always been kind of fucked up, though.

"I care," my dad says. "I'm so sorry. I... I don't even know what to say. I'm sorry, Ethan."

He hugs me and I hug him back. It's rough and rugged, like we're two burly lumberjacks, except I'm pretty sure lumberjacks don't bawl onto each other's shoulders. We're in the woods, though. Just the middle of the woods, in the middle of nowhere, and it's not like anyone can see us. It's getting kind of dark out, too. How long have we been out here?

Fuck if I know.

Everything's going pretty good, I guess. I think. I don't know. Can I tell him about Ashley now? Nah, it's not even a good time anymore. Why the fuck did I bring this shit up? How am I supposed to tell him by the time we get back if I just fucking dropped this bomb on him? He did it, too, though. It's not just my bomb to drop, it's ours, together.

I guess we should have done this a long time ago, but I'm not sure how we could have.

We separate, but we keep looking at each other. I feel like my dad's a different person now, and he's looking at me like I'm different, too.

We're not that different, though. I mean, shit, I'm still a huge fuck up. I've still done a lot of stupid shit, slept with a ton of girls, broke their hearts. I didn't exactly mean to, and most of the time I was trying to help them and show them a good time because they deserved it, even if just for a little while. I wasn't good for them, and I knew that, but they didn't. How the fuck do you tell someone that?

I guess that's what my dad was doing for me, too, though. This is really hard to deal with. It's like some giant epiphany or something. We both did things in our own ways, but we were trying to do what we thought was right.

Can I forgive him? I don't know, can he forgive me? Is that what this is even about?

We keep walking quietly, and I know now that neither of us has any clue where we're going. It just seems like the right thing to do. Walk it off, you know?

My football coach used to say that we were either hurt, or in pain. If you're hurt, you need to go see a doctor. If you're just in pain, you need to suck it up, walk it off, and get back to practice.

I used to be hurt. I'm just in pain right now. I'll get over it. Whatever doesn't kill you only makes you stronger, right? Yeah yeah, I think that's kind of a bunch of bullshit, but whatever. Maybe it's true.

I think what just happened between me and my dad will help us, though. Maybe. Fuck if I know. I'm not a psychologist. Maybe Ashley will know, but I'm pretty sure she's not a psychologist, either. Shit, this is difficult.

When the fuck did it get so dark out? It's not night yet, but it's almost dusk, and here we are, just walking in the fucking woods. Shit, it's been hours.

"I'm not sure where we are," my dad says.

I shrug. "Me either."

"We should turn back," he says. "We should be able to retrace our steps before it gets too dark. We don't want to be stuck in the woods like this at night."

Yeah, and that's a real good idea, except there's one small problem.

I guess it's not a small problem, but a potentially pretty big one.

We turn around to head back, and a few seconds after we hear a howl. Fuck. It sounds close, too. Like... not even joking here, I wouldn't be surprised if you said the howl was right behind us.

My dad freezes, and so do I. Yeah...

The campground owner told us there were reports of wolves in the woods, but he said it was just a rumor and nothing was confirmed. Oh yeah? Well, guess what? I think we just confirmed it.

"Shit," my dad says.

"Yup..."

6 - Ashley

I SAW ASHLEY AND ETHAN in the woods," Caleb blurts out. "Uh... and her shorts were off and Ethan's hand was in her underwear, and they were kissing, and... oh my God I can't believe I just said that in front of your mom I'm so sorry."

My mom furrows her brow, listening intently to Caleb. When he stops talking, she turns to me, brow still furrowed. She purses her lips and shakes her head at me.

"Ashley?" she says, sighing. "Really, now? In the middle of the woods?"

I don't think I should tell her what Ethan and I were doing in the middle of the woods just a little earlier after Caleb saw us. But, really, it's the middle of the woods! It's called that for a reason, isn't it? I feel like people should be able to expect some small amount of privacy when they're in the middle of the woods compared to the middle of somewhere else. If Ethan and I were in the middle of a shopping mall, for example, well... I could understand why that might be a cause for concern.

What if it's in a photo booth in the middle of the shopping mall, though? That sounds like something Ethan would do, and I feel like I need to prepare for a situation like that. It's better to be prepared than have these sorts of things sprung on you without warning, isn't it?

I'm pretty sure my mom won't be agreeing with me any time soon. She's still looking at me with a slightly concerned look on her face. Yes, well... *yes*.

I turn to Caleb and frown at him. "I thought you said you weren't going to say anything?" I tell him.

"Oh," he says. "Um... I didn't mean to?"

"You sort of just did, though! I'm not very happy with you, Caleb."

"Sorry..." he says, looking away, shy. Then he realizes what he's apologizing for and he turns back, confused. "Wait, this isn't my fault! You're the one having... uh... you were... with Ethan... it wasn't exactly sex, I guess, but..." Then, fast, he blurts out. "Ashley, that's your brother! That's kind of gross, don't you think?"

"Ohhh," my mom says, as if she's finally understanding the issue here, or Caleb's issue at least. Sometimes my mom is weird. "I see what the problem is. Caleb, Ethan is actually Ashley's step-brother."

"Er...?" Caleb glances quickly between me and my mom.

"We're not related, you dweeb!" I tell him.

I'm still angry, too. It's just my mom, and it's not a huge deal that he told her, but I don't exactly appreciate being caught out like that, either. I would have preferred my mother not know about what Ethan and I were attempting to do in private, you know?

"Oh... uh... sorry?" Caleb says. After a second's pause, he adds, "Really, he's your stepbrother? How long?"

"Um, a few years now? Almost four, I guess. We've only been dating for a little over a week, though," I add. "It's kind of a secret, but I guess you know now."

"He's the guy you were talking about at the store? You're boyfriend?"

"Yup, that's him. So you can see why you need to keep it a secret, except I don't even know if I can trust you with secrets anymore, Caleb."

"No! You can!" He sounds so adamant about it. "I... honestly, I was confused and surprised and I didn't mean to say that in front of your mom. I won't tell anyone else. It's just, you really shouldn't do that in the woods. You were being kind of loud and someone else might have heard you. I'm not sure how you would have explained that to my dad. We're supposed to be a family friendly camp-ground."

"Oh, I'm sure Ethan and Ashley were being *very* friendly," my mom says, grinning.

"Mom! Seriously?" I stare at her, pointed. She just looks at me and shrugs. "Wow."

"Lots of people just use the showers," Caleb adds. "For alone time, I mean. You just can't make it obvious what's going on in there, but there's no real rules against two people showering at the same time. Plenty of people just take showers in their bathing suits with someone else to save money. My dad doesn't mind as long as no one complains."

"Oh, I'm pretty sure they've already used the showers," my mom says, shaking her head.

She's really having fun with this, isn't she? I thought she was supposed to be my friend and, well, my mother, but here she is, just teasing me without remorse. Ugh.

"Mom," I say, staring at her. "Really?"

"Go ahead and tell me you weren't in the shower with Ethan this morning, dear. If you can say it with a straight face and promise you aren't lying, I'll believe you."

I huff and turn away from her, crossing my arms over my chest. My fishing pole lays discarded on the ground and I kind of glare at it, but there's not even a worm on the hook so what do I care?

Caleb just stares at us, dumbfounded. I'm not sure he's ever met a family like ours, and, um... I don't think I've met a family like ours, either? This is kind of bad, isn't it? I never meant for this to happen, it just sort of happened, and I wish I could blame Ethan, but the shower part was entirely my plan.

"Do you want to fish with us, Caleb?" my mom asks him. "I think we're going to be here for awhile. We're waiting for the boys to come back, but you're welcome to join us if you'd like?"

"Is that alright?" he asks us. "You're not mad at me?"

"I'm not mad, honey," she says to him, smiling. "Are you, Ashley?"

"I'm kind of mad," I say, mumbling.

"Are you mad at Caleb or are you mad that you and Ethan got caught?"

Why does she have to ask questions like that? I wish I could lie to my mother, but I just can't. I don't even know if I can really lie to anyone. It's hard. Maybe Ethan can, but I have a difficult time trying to do it, especially when I'm dealing with my mom.

"I'm sorry," I say. "You shouldn't have said that in front of my mom, Caleb, but it was kind of my fault, too."

"Sorry," Caleb says. "I can see why you like Ethan, though. He's really cool."

Ethan's cool? Yup, I guess so, but I never really thought of it like that.

"Ethan and Ashley have some growing up to do," my mom says. "They're both wonderful people, but this is their first real relationship, and those can be difficult sometimes. We're still trying to figure out how to tell Ethan's father, but I think we'll have that out of the way soon. Then hopefully these two won't feel the need to sneak off into the woods to spend time alone together."

"Um, I'm pretty sure we might," I tell my mom before I think about what I'm saying. "It's not like we can go in the tent with you and his dad right outside."

"Really," my mom says. "How often do you two need alone time?"

"Um... I don't want to answer that."

How do you even answer a question like that? I feel like, if we're taking Ethan's whims into account, it's at least once a day, but then if we're adding my whims, it's maybe twice, except sometimes we each have half a whim and when you add those together, it's a full whim, so three times.

Really, this is a complex algebraic problem that requires multiple equations to solve.

Except if I say that out loud I just sound like some kind of sex freak. Ethan can sound like a sex freak and I guess that's fine, but I'm not supposed to be a sex freak. I kind of like being a sex freak, but I don't think I'm supposed to admit that to anyone, so I'm not going to. I'm just not.

My mom rolls her eyes at me, and then she beckons Caleb over.

"Let's see about fishing, shall we?" she says to him. "Do you have a girlfriend, Caleb?"

7 - Ethan

YEAH, SO, WE'RE FUCKED. Completely fucking screwed. Lost in the woods, no big deal, except it's a pretty fucking big deal because there's wolves or something. We haven't seen them yet, but that's not exactly a good consolation here, because every so often we hear a howl, and I think it's getting closer.

Look, I don't know exactly what a wolf sounds like, so I couldn't tell you if this is multiple wolves or one wolf or a baby wolf or whatever the fuck. I literally do not know, and to be honest I don't give a fuck what's going on there wherever the fuck the wolf or wolves are. I just don't want to get eaten by a wolf.

Maybe I'm a bad boy and you think I should just like... fight the wolf or something? Are you serious, though? Who the fuck fights a wolf? You think this wolf is just going to bow down to my greatness? Shit, how awesome would that be, though? Yeah, just walk out, see a wolf, he puts two paws to the ground, lowers his muzzle, and submits to my badassery.

If Ashley were here she'd yell at me for trying to make badassery into a word. You know what? It's a pretty amazing word if I do say so myself.

Anyways, that's where we're at. Woods, lost, wolf, running, and holy fuck.

Yup...

We try to retrace our steps, but it's getting darker and it's hard to see. We can still technically see, but I think we overstayed our welcome in here. The forest is not our friend, and that's becoming more and more obvious with each passing minute.

"Here," my dad says, sidestepping past a tree and heading towards a hillside.

There's a small cave here. Nothing huge, but we can hide out in there. Except it's a mother-fucking wolf. You think it's not going to find us in this cave? Pretty fucking sure that's exactly what wolves do.

Whatever. I guess we can at least defend our-selves in here better.

My dad heads to the back of the cave, which is to say it's only maybe a few steps in. He sighs and leans against the back, sliding to the ground. I sit next to him, watching the entrance.

"We're completely fucking screwed, huh?" I say.

"Ethan," my dad says. "Don't say stuff like that."

"How's this going to work then?" I tell him. "Do you think we can get out of here or what? Because I sure don't."

"It's just a wolf," my dad says. "It's probably not even interested in us."

I laugh. I don't mean to laugh, but does he know what he's saying? Just a wolf? Uh... pretty fucking sure a wolf could destroy us.

I'm a pretty tough guy, alright? I lift weights, I know what's up. Yeah, I'm a quarterback, so techni-cally speaking I don't get into too many fights on the field, but I like to run the ball as much as I like handing it off or passing it, and if you're going to run with it, you've got to be able to not only take a hit, but sometimes give one out, too.

Football isn't some fancypants ballet or any-thing, it's a legitimate contact sport, and sometimes you've just got to knock a fucker to the ground. I mean that in a nice way.

That's with people, though. Human beings. I'm not going to tackle a fucking wolf. I mean, if I really have to, I guess I'll give it a shot, but it's not my idea of a good time.

"I'm sorry," my dad says. "I'm not sure how this happened. We should have just stayed on the trail. I thought it'd be fun to head out on our own."

"Yeah... like we used to," I say.

The first time we went camping, we both pissed each other off. We wouldn't talk to each other, but it's hard not to talk to someone when you're stuck in a tent five feet away from them. It's even harder when you rely on each other for everything, and there's nothing else to do. No TV, no video games, no friends or anywhere to go. It's the fucking woods, alright?

"I know it wasn't much, but I liked hiking with you," my dad says to me.

"Yeah, I liked it, too," I say.

It was a lot, though. It was the first time in a long time where I thought maybe my dad actually cared about me.

I was the one who said we shouldn't follow the regular hiking trails. I was always doing things to try and get a rise out of him, to see if he would say anything. Usually he didn't even bother, he just let me do whatever. I honestly felt like he didn't care anymore.

When I suggested we head off into the woods without a destination or a path, my dad agreed, though. Sure, he said. Why not?

And... it was really fun.

We sit next to each other now, and stay quiet, listening. After a few more minutes, we hear another howl. It sounds closer, but also different. Confused or something? Fuck if I know. It's a wolf.

"Maybe it's a friendly wolf," I suggest with a shrug. "Like in a Disney movie or something."

My dad laughs. It's louder than I expected, and it makes me laugh, too. We're really fucked here, but it's nice that we can laugh together.

"What Disney movie has friendly wolves?" my dad asks. "Mice, dragons, and lions, sure, but wolves?"

"Shit," I say, laughing. "You're right."

My dad laughs again. "Ah, well."

"Hey," I say to him, quiet. "Can I tell you something?"

"If it's some deathbed confession, save it," he says. "We're going to be fine."

Yeah, well...

"Nah," I say. "That's not it."

"What is it?" he asks.

"I like you and Ashley's mom together," I say. "I think you two are good for each other and I really like her, too. I know maybe this doesn't mean much, because I fuck up a lot of the time, but I love you, Dad, and I want you to be happy, and I'm glad you're happy with her."

My dad stays silent for awhile. I don't know if he's thinking of something to say or if I've said enough for the both of us. After awhile, we hear more noises. It's getting closer. I can hear the rustling of an animal in the forest outside of our cave. I don't even fucking know if you could consider this a cave, to be honest. It's a fucking small hole in a hill and it's not protecting us from shit, least of all a wolf.

"Thanks," my dad says. "That means a lot. I *am* happy, Ethan, but I want you to be happy, too."

"Do you really mean it or are you just saying that?" I ask him.

"Ethan, of course I mean it," he says.

Yeah, well, it's now or never. And by that I mean we're about to get attacked by a wolf or something, so...

I can hear it and see it standing there in front of us. It's dusk and dark and I can't see much besides the glint of yellow in its eyes and the white shine of its teeth. My dad bristles and tenses, preparing for action. What kind of action do you even take in a situation like this. I move to stand a little, but I think I'd probably be better served with a kick.

Fuck if I know why. Just seems easier to kick a wolf than to punch it, don't you think? What, you want me to drag the wolf into a headlock and choke it out or something? Nah...

Alright, so, now or never. I'm not going to hold off anymore. No more procrastinating or waiting for the perfect moment because I don't know if I'll have any more moments after this.

"I love Ashley," I tell him. "We've been dating. That's who it is. My girlfriend. I was scared to tell you because I know you're going to think it's stupid and you think I'm going to fuck it up and I can't say I blame you because I think I'm going to fuck it up, too. I don't want to, though. I'm serious about this, Dad. I want to be with her, and, uh... fuck, I can't even do this anymore. I..."

The wolf is getting closer. I kick my foot out before it gets too close and it backs off and sits on its haunches, staring at us.

"...You and Ashley?" my dad asks. "Are you serious? Ethan, she's..."

"Yeah, yeah. Fuck! I know, alright? She's my stepsister. I get it. What's that even mean, though? Not a whole fucking lot. I never meant for this to happen. I've liked her for awhile now, but I know what kind of person I am and... look, why are we even doing this? I don't have to explain myself, and there's a fucking wolf right here, so, uh... just, yeah."

Except this is one really fucked up wolf. It howls again, lonely, just acting like it owns the place. Maybe it does. How fucked up would that be? We try to hide, but we enter the den of a wolf. Cool. Good fucking job. Go, us!

"What the fuck are you howling at?" I say to the wolf, because, you know, usually you expect wolves to answer your questions, right?

The fucking wolf barks at me. Seriously it barks. And it keeps barking.

My dad stares at it. I stare at it, too. Wait a second...

"You're not even a fucking wolf!" I yell at it.

It barks again, excited.

"Is that a dog?" my dad asks.

Yeah, fuck you, we were running away from a dog. You want to make something of it? If you hear a dog howling in the dark in the middle of the woods, you'd run away, too.

But, seriously, it could be a wild dog or something. Just because it's a dog, doesn't mean that...

Nah, this dog just lies down and stares at us. Fucking dog...

"Are you a nice dog or what?" I ask it.

It barks and starts panting at us.

"Well, get the fuck over here and let me pet you then!"

Look, I'm real good with dogs, alright? Don't you forget it.

The dog comes, though. It even holds out his paw.

"I'm not falling for that," I tell him. "I shake your hand then you bite me? Nah."

He flops onto his side and then rolls on his back.

"Alright, so maybe you aren't that dangerous."

He barks at me, excited, so I reach out and pat his stomach. I guess he likes that because he starts wriggling closer to me, then nudges his head against my foot.

"Come here," my dad says.

The dog gets up and sits on his back legs in front of us. We both take a good look at him. It's dark, but he's close, so it's easier.

And, yeah, he's kind of scary looking for a dog? German shepherd mix from the looks of it, so kind of wolf-like already, but those kinds of dogs get a bad rap for no reason a lot of the time. I'm kind of glad we found him, then. What would happen if some hunter saw him, and, uh... yup... not good.

"You're coming with us," I tell him.

He barks at me.

"Yeah, you like that, huh?"

"Ethan, we can't take him with us," my dad says.

"What, why not?" I ask.

"Uh... it's a dog?" he says.

"What the fuck kind of reason is that?" No, seriously, what the fuck?

"He could have fleas. In all likelihood he has fleas. He might even have an owner. Look, there's a collar right there."

"There's no tags, though," I point out, reaching for the collar and twisting it around. "It's dirty and old, too."

"We should bring him to an animal shelter, at least," my dad says. "This isn't a good place for him."

"Yeah, except we're lost," I add.

The dog barks. Now that he's got friends, he sure does like to bark. What was with the howling before? Maybe he was just lonely. It's cool, dog. I totally understand. I'd be lonely if I was lost in the woods, too.

The dog gets up and starts trying to lead us away or something.

"Are you Lassie or what?" I ask him.

He barks. I think that's dog for "Yes" but what the fuck do I know?

"Let's try to find our way back before it gets a lot darker," my dad says.

"Yeah," I say. "That's probably a good idea."

"And, Ethan?"

"Yeah?"

"Were you serious about you and Ashley before? What you said to me?"

"Yeah," I say. I don't know what else to say. I don't want to say more than that. I don't expect him to understand or agree with me, but I just want him to know.

"It's a lot to take in," my dad says. "Let's talk about it tomorrow. After we get back to the campsite, alright? It's too much for today, but I want to talk to you about it."

"Alright," I say.

I don't know if that's good or bad. I guess it's better than being eaten by a wolf, at any rate.

Pretty fucking sure I'm just being slobbered on by this dog, though. I reach out to pet him and he starts licking me and drooling all over my hand.

"Seriously?" I say to him. "That's gross."

We leave the cave and use the dwindling light of a fading sunset to make our way back to the makeshift path we were following. One thing that's nice is the darker it gets, the easier it is to make out any lights that are nearby. Which... yeah, well, there's none nearby, but I think there's some way over there, far ahead of us in the woods. Hopefully that means a campsite. Or evil faeries planning to lead us to our doom.

Fucking evil faeries, man... seriously, what kind of bullshit is that? Just pisses me off.

Also, holy shit, I think I just heard another howl. Pretty sure my dad did, too, and the dog's ears perk up.

"Uh... let's go," my dad says. "Now."

"Yeah, good idea," I say to him.

Mia Clark

8 - Ashley

C ALEB BECOMES OUR FISHING HELPER and ends up baiting all of our hooks. I'm not sure this is what he had in mind when he first showed up here, but he seems fine with it. It's actually kind of weird to me, because it's so different from how Ethan is. Caleb is helpful and nice, and I don't want to say that Ethan isn't helpful or nice, but, um...

I guess Ethan is, but in a different way? He's more of the commanding, take charge sort, while Caleb seems content to just help out with whatever someone needs help with. Which maybe my mom and I are using to our advantage right now, but Caleb seems to be enjoying himself, too.

Also, Caleb has a secret. Oh, yes, it's a very good secret, too.

He tried to avoid my mom's scrutinizing questions about him having a girlfriend, but my mom is really good at this kind of thing and Caleb couldn't guard himself for very long. He does not have a girlfriend, but...

"There is this one girl," Caleb says. "Uh... her name is Scarlet."

"Oh?" my mom asks. "How did you meet her?"

"She's my neighbor," Caleb says. "Back home, I mean. Not here. She's never been to the campground, though I've told her all about it."

"Is she interested?" my mom asks.

"You could invite her?" I add.

"Oh, er... no, I couldn't do that..." Caleb says.

A fish bites at my hook and I try to, um... fish it? I don't know! This is my first time fishing and honestly I have no idea what I'm supposed to be doing. A second later, it's no longer nibbling at the end of my line, though. I reel in the line and check and it's just eaten my worm and vanished!

Actually, I'm relieved. I know we're supposed to be fishing, but I feel bad for the fish. Thankfully neither of us has caught any fish whatsoever, so mostly we're just feeding them worms. I feel like there's worse ways to spend your day. Plenty of people go to the park to feed the birds, right? This is like the same thing, except we're at a lake feeding the fish.

"Why can't you?" I ask Caleb while he baits a worm on my hook for me.

"This is going to sound weird," Caleb says. "Uh... Scarlet kind of reminds me of Ethan?"

"Oh," my mom says, nodding in complete understanding. "She's the bad girl type, is she?"

Caleb starts to blush. "Well, er... I don't... I don't know about that, uh..."

I suddenly feel an urgent need to help Caleb. I don't know why, I just... I want to help him. He's like me, isn't he? And I needed Ethan as my bad boy to show me what I was capable of. Caleb needs his bad girl, too. I think he does. Oh no, what if he doesn't? What if Scarlet isn't like Ethan at all and she's going to be mean to Caleb and treat him poorly?

Because, to be honest, I don't think all bad boys are good. Just Ethan, really. Actually, I don't even know because I've never really dealt with any besides him. I wouldn't consider Jake a bad boy, despite the fact that he's kind of a jerk. That's not what being a bad boy means, you know? It's completely different, and now I'm not sure how I feel about Scarlet.

"She's an art student," Caleb says, wistful. "She just started college last year. Well, I did, too, actually. I kind of maybe sort of applied to the college across the street from hers, because, uh... well, we hang out sometimes, but I'm not really like all of those other art school kids. I'm not as cool, I guess."

"No way," I say. "I think you're cool, Caleb. I bet she does, too. Why else would she hang out with you?"

Caleb shrugs. "I don't know? Because we've known each other forever, I guess. I don't think she hangs out with me for any other reason than that."

"I think you're wrong," I say. "Do you have her number?"

"Er... yes?"

"We're going to call her," I say. "What's she doing this summer? Is she home?"

"Probably, but I bet she's working on some big art project. She does lots of painting. She's really good."

I want to say more, and I fully planned on saying more, but it's getting dark and something stops me. We don't have much time left before the sun sets, and we really should be heading back. I think my mom and I are only staying now because we figured Ethan and his dad would be back soon. I'm trying not to worry, but Ethan did say he was going to tell his dad while they were on their hike, and it's hard not to worry about that.

What if something happened? What if his dad got so upset that he stormed off and they're lost in the woods now, and something bad happened? Maybe they fell into a hole and they got trapped and they're stuck. Maybe Ethan broke his leg, or his dad broke his leg, or they both broke their legs, and...

Really, that's a little too much worrying, but the only reason I started worrying about all of this so suddenly was the howling. Before I could toss my freshly baited hook into the water, a piercing howl echoes through the woods across the lake.

We all freeze: me, Caleb, and my mother.

"Oh, shit," Caleb says. "I didn't think there'd actually be a wolf."

"Wait, what?" I ask. "Are you serious?"

"It did sound like a wolf," my mom says. "That's not good, now is it?"

"Where did you say Ethan and his dad were going?" Caleb asks.

"Just for a hike, I guess? I'm not sure," I say.

"I thought they'd be back by now," my mom adds. "It's been quite a few hours, I think. We sort of lost track of time. I don't have a watch."

Caleb checks his watch. "It's almost sunset," he says. "I'm not sure how long you've been out here, but I've been with you for about three hours."

"What? Seriously?" Holy wow, three hours? Um...

The wolf howls again. Or, possibly worse, another wolf howls?

"We need to find them," I say. "We need to go get them before it's dark."

"It's not that easy," Caleb says. "If you don't know where they went, and we have no way of contacting them, it's going to be really difficult to find them. For all we know, they could be back at the campsite by now, too. Maybe they're heading back now."

"I'm sure they're fine..." my mom says, but she doesn't even sound like she believes her own words.

"We should probably head back, too," Caleb says. "If there's a wolf out here, it's not safe. We put out scent markers to deter most animals from getting too close to the campground, but we mostly keep it to this side of the lake. Most wild animals won't bother you during the day, and the scent markers mostly keep them away at night, but..."

He doesn't have to explain more. If there's wolves in the woods and there's nothing to stop them, then anyone caught near them could be in trouble. I'm not sure how aggressive wolves usually are to humans, but I'm sure if a pack of them catches two lone hikers in the middle of the woods...

I don't even want to think about it. *Please be alright.* I know my stepdad and Ethan can usually take care of themselves, but I'm worried. Please... *please be alright.*

9 - Ethan

THESE FUCKING WOODS. Seriously, super real talk right now, but what the fuck is up with these woods? We saw lights before, but they weren't even real lights. I mean, I guess they were *lights* in the strictest sense of the word, but who the fuck needs fireflies when you're lost in the woods?

Also, we've got this dog with us, and it's not even helpful. It just keeps circling around us, over and over, running in circles...

Yup, thanks, Dog. Thanks a lot.

Maybe I should give it a name or something? What the fuck, he's not even my dog, though. He should have a name already.

The next time he comes close, I hold out my hand to pet him and he stops. I reach for his collar, but that's all there is, no tags, nothing. He looks at me with contented eyes, his tongue lolling out of his mouth.

"Kind of strange that there's a dog out here, huh?" my dad asks.

"Uh, yeah," I say.

My dad laughs. "I thought we were done for before."

"Yeah..." Yeah, I did, too.

"I'm not sure if it's because of that or something else, but I'm glad you told me," he says.

"Told you what?" I ask. I'm not trying to be stupid here, but I want to make sure I know what he's talking about.

"You," he says. "And Ashley. It makes sense now. I'm not sure why I didn't see it before. I guess I just never thought of it as a possibility. You two have gotten on each other's nerves for such a long time, you know?"

"Yeah, I know," I say. "I really do like her, though. This isn't a fling or anything, Dad."

It isn't a fling now. It was going to be a fling when we first started our "with benefits" arrangement, but to be honest I'm not even sure if it was a fling then.

I loved how she challenged me. I mean, I didn't have to give in, you know? I could have pushed back, told her she was just drunk, saying stupid shit. Yeah, yeah, that first fateful fucking night when she dared me to sleep with her. She wanted to win, and I know she might not have thought that through entirely. You don't just say shit like that unless you mean it, though.

Maybe she didn't think I would do it, and maybe that's why she said it in the first place, but I think a part of her wanted it. I think a part of her just wanted to know what it was like. Maybe she thought it'd be fine to do it just for one night, and... fuck, that wouldn't have been fine with me. That's why I suggested the whole stepbrother with benefits thing in the first place.

I gave her a way out, though. I told her we could stop. I wasn't the one that chose this. I would have fucking chose it if someone gave me the choice, though.

I don't know if I deserve Ashley. I really fucking don't. She probably deserves someone better than me. Someone like Caleb, maybe. He seems like an alright guy, though kind of a pussy. Needs to man up a little, but other than that, he's not the worst.

I don't know what the fuck I'm saying anymore except that I want to be good for Ashley. I know I'm not exactly the kind of guy a mother wants dating her daughter, but I want to be. I don't think my dad is wrong about that. I don't think he was wrong to say that if Ashley was his daughter, he wouldn't want me dating her.

It's just...

It's a challenge, too, you know? It's like Ashley's dare, except this is my life, and I want to do it, and I want to win.

Winning means forever. Happily fucking ever after. It means love and romance and all the shit I never really thought about before, because I never thought I'd have it. I wanted other people to find it and have it, but do you know how fucking hard that is?

Falling in love isn't easy. I mean *really* falling in love. Not lust or temporary satisfaction or settling for someone who is nice to you. There's nothing wrong with that, either, don't get me wrong. Sometimes lust can become love. I mean, fuck, that's kind of what happened with me and Ashley, isn't it? Sometimes friendship can become love, too. I think that's what happened, also.

I just want everything. Love, lust, friendship, and a whole lot more. Ashley is everything. She's so fucking good at all of it, and it makes me want to be better.

I mean, yeah, I want to be a bad boy, too, but I think she likes that. I just kind of want to be a bad boy and boyfriend material at the same time. Maybe husband and father material, too, but let's not get too carried away here.

I have a lot of time to think about this shit. Me and my dad are just walking, and this dog is walking with us, too. I think maybe we're heading back to the campsite, but I have no fucking clue.

My dad clears his throat. I think that's it, but then he opens his mouth to talk.

"I love you, Ethan," he says. "No matter what, I want you to know I love you, alright?"

"Yeah," I say.

It's not like I was going to say more. I have no idea what to say right now. I just want to get back to the campsite and to Ashley and then we can deal with this shit, or just wait until tomorrow. Sleep on it, right? Yeah, sounds good.

Except, nah, nothing is that easy. Nothing is ever that fucking easy.

The dog pulls back and bristles, but whatever the fuck it sees, I sure can't see it. Then, out of nowhere, there's this huge fucking bear. Black like the descending night, just hiding behind a fucking tree or some shit. This isn't a fake bear, not a dog that looks like a bear. A bear is a fucking bear, and there's no real way for someone to mistake it for something else.

I mean, I guess it could be Bigfoot, too, but let's not get too carried away here.

It makes a loud, guttural noise and stands up on its hind legs, aggressive. Thank fuck it's a decent distance away from of us. Like... not that far ahead, but at least we're not within arm's reach of it. I'm not sure this is going to help much, because it's a fucking bear and if it wants to have us for dinner, well... yeah, it's only got to take a few steps forward.

The dog starts barking, though. Then, no shit, it lunges at the bear.

"What the fuck are you doing?" I scream at the dog.

A whole lot of fucking good that does me. Try asking a dog what the fuck it's doing sometime and tell me what happens? Here, I'll just tell you what happens now so you don't have to.

Nothing. The dog doesn't give a fuck. It's a fucking dog and it's attacking this bear. Holy shit.

My dad jumps back as if to protect me, which is cool and all except this bear is massive and I'm pretty sure it could take us both down. The dog leaps forward and barks at the bear and then dashes to the side. The bear looks confused for a second, then falls back to the ground, on both legs again. The dog doubles back, standing in front of me and my dad, then it barks and growls at the bear again.

Apparently bears don't like when you bark and growl at them. Or jump towards them. I don't recommend jumping on a bear, or barking and growling at it, but if that's all you've got left between you and your imminent demise, then, yeah, fuck it, why not?

It worked for the dog, so who am I to judge?

The bear lets out one last grunt, which is kind of a yelp, too, and then it turns around quick and runs back into the woods.

"Holy shit," my dad says.

I agree with him. "Holy fucking shit."

The dog doesn't say anything, he just looks real fucking pleased with himself. Tongue lolling out of his mouth, staring at us like we're his best friends.

You know what? Yeah, I want this dog to be my best friend.

"You're kind of dumb, aren't you?" I ask the dog. "You think that was smart or what? You could have gotten eaten by a bear."

"Ethan, why are you talking to the dog?" my dad asks.

I don't know? Because? The dog barks at me like he's saying it's totally cool to talk to dogs. This dog knows what's up.

"Yeah, alright, you can chase off bears, but how the fuck do we get out of the woods?" I ask him.

My dad thinks I'm crazy. I think I'm crazy, too, but I'd rather be crazy and talking to a dog than stuck in the woods for the night. There's fucking bears out here, man.

That's when it happens, too. I guess this is a turning point in my life. I don't know what it means, and I'm not sure what turned, but...

"Do you hear that?" my dad asks.

The dog barks. He totally hears it.

"I'm not talking to you," my dad says to the dog.

The dog barks. I don't think he likes my dad. I guess I can't blame him, because sometimes I don't like my dad, either, but he's not so bad.

"Sounds like the river," I say. "Maybe the lake? I don't know. It's water, at least. That's a good sign."

"Yeah, let's see if we can find it. We should be able to get back to the campsite then."

"Yeah, fucking... I hope so," I say. "Sorry about swearing so much."

My dad laughs. "I don't think I've ever told you this, but I kind of like it when you do. Do you know how often I want to curse at people when I'm working? I've got to maintain my composure and act professional, but sometimes people, they..." He pauses for a second. "They do really stupid shit and I want to tell them that."

I laugh. This is new and interesting. I didn't know my dad was a badass in the making.

"I envy you sometimes, Ethan," he says, smiling. "Not always. Don't get the wrong idea here. You're young and free and a little reckless, but I think you can go far if you learn how to temper your willfulness sometimes. Not too much, but you take risks that other people wouldn't even dare to take."

"Yeah, well, sometimes I fuck up really bad, though," I say.

"We all fuck up really bad sometimes," my dad says. "It's a balancing act. You can't always play it safe, and you can't always take risks. That's why--"

He stops. He just doesn't want to say more, I guess. I think I know what he's going to say, and it makes me smile, but it's too dark for him to see it. I think he's smiling, too, though.

"We'll talk about this in the morning," he says. "Let's go home."

Home. It's not a building or an exact area. It's the place where people are waiting for us. It's where Ashley and her mom are. Whether it's in the city, back in our mansion, or in the middle of these woods at the campsite.

That's where our home is. That's where we belong.

Sometimes we fuck up, but we've got a safe place to go back to. It's safe because of who's there waiting for us.

Yeah, I like that. Let's go home, Dad.

10 - Ashley

IT'S DARK NOW AND they aren't back yet. We haven't heard any more wolf howling, but that was at the lake, so it makes sense we wouldn't hear it at our campsite. I'm not exactly sure how far away the lake is from the campground, but I think it's at least a mile or so.

Caleb stayed with us, and I guess I'm thankful, but I don't really know. He started a fire for me and my mom and then he helped my mom make a quick dinner for all of us. His dad stopped by for a little and said he'd call the forest ranger or something like that. I don't even know how this works.

"Can they go look for them?" I ask Caleb. I don't know who *they* is, but I just want someone to find Ethan and his dad.

"Searching in the woods at night isn't really useful," Caleb says. "It's a lot harder. Usually the search and rescue teams will just wait until morning. It's really hard to see in the woods at night, especially when you have to be extra careful about where you're going. They can cover a lot more ground during the day."

"I'm sure everything will be fine, honey," my mom says.

We made quick mac and cheese for dinner, along with grilling some chicken breasts. My mom wrapped them in tinfoil and then put them on top of the grate that Ethan's dad brought. They're nice and juicy, seasoned with a few local grown spices, and usually I'd love it, but...

I like mac and cheese, too. There's still some more keeping warm on the edge of the cooking grate, but I don't want to eat it. No one else does, either. It's kind of an unspoken agreement that it's there for Ethan and his dad when they come back... if they come back.

"What could happen to them?" I ask.

I'm not sure who I'm asking. Caleb, I guess. My mom knows as much about camping as I do, which is, um... not much at all.

Caleb doesn't answer, and I don't like the way he looks over at me. I don't want him to look at me like that. I don't even want him to look at me at all. I think he's nice and all, but I should be here with Ethan. We're supposed to be enjoying a family camping trip, but he's not even here. Seriously, what a jerk!

I'm angry, but I don't want to be angry. I'm angry at myself, I guess. I'm angry that I didn't just tell Ethan's dad about us this morning when I was in the shower. I could have. I could have told him any number of times before now.

It's stupid. We're stupid. Why did we think this was a good idea? We tried to hide it, but look what good that did us? Maybe if we'd just told his dad right when he got home, everything would have been fine. I don't know. Even if it wasn't fine, at least we'd be safe. I'd rather Ethan's dad be mad at us than for him and Ethan to be...

No, I can't think like that. They're fine. I'm sure they're fine. It's just...

I watch my mom, and I realize I'm angry at her, too. She could have told Ethan's dad. She said she would when they were on a trip together. She said that she'd tell him before they came home, but then she didn't.

Maybe this is stupid, but I'm really mad at Ethan, too. He didn't tell me he liked me before. I don't even know if he did. He says he did, says he's liked me for a long time, but then why didn't he ever tell me? Why did he wait until just last week to sort of admit it. He didn't even admit it, though.

What would have happened if he never admitted it? If we did our stepbrother with benefits thing for the week and then stopped and went our separate ways?

This is stupid. I'm projecting or something. I'm trying to find a place for my anger, but I'm not even really angry, I'm...

I'm scared. I'm so very scared. I hope they're fine. I really really hope so, but there's nothing I can do and no way I can tell, which just makes me more scared.

I hear someone coming towards our campsite, but I don't bother looking up. It's probably Caleb's dad coming for him. It's not like Caleb can stay here with us. We don't have a tent for him. He has his own place, too. He's got his own home, and his own family, and his own...

"Fuck, man... is that chicken and mac and cheese?"

"Looks like it's still warm, too."

Um... Ethan? And my stepfather?

I look up to see them both standing there. For some reason, there's a dog with them, too. The dog stares at us: me, my mom, and Caleb. When he sees the leftovers on my paper dinner plate, he runs over and starts licking it clean. I don't even care, I can't take my eyes off of Ethan.

He looks at me, too, but then he looks away, kind of shy or embarrassed? His dad elbows him, nudging him forward, and Ethan takes a step towards me.

I'm done. I lose it. I jump up and run across the campsite to Ethan. He looks confused at first, but then he's smiling. I leap into his arms and he catches me. I wrap my legs around his waist and my arms around his neck and he squeezes me close and holds me tight, his arms around my butt.

We're practically standing right next to his dad, but I don't even care. I kiss Ethan. I shower his face with kisses, my lips touching every inch of him that I can find. There, there, there... his nose, his cheeks, his eyes.

His lips.

He kisses me back, too. This is getting, um... it's kind of hot, which is kind of awkward, because we're just right out in the open. Caleb is staring at us, wide-eyed and open-mouthed. Ethan's dad goes over to my mom and hugs her tight, whispering something to her.

When Ethan and I finally stop kissing, he glances over at Caleb.

"What the fuck are you doing here?" he asks.

"Uh...?" Caleb blushes and looks away.

"Ethan, be nice," I tell him. "Caleb was worried about you, too, you know?"

"Oh yeah?" Ethan asks, brow furrowed. "You weren't flirting with Ashley, were you?"

"N-no!" Caleb says, flustered.

I whisper to Ethan. "Caleb has a crush on a girl named Scarlet. I thought we could help him, maybe?"

"Uh... what?" Now Ethan looks confused and sort of flustered. It's kind of cute and makes me laugh.

"I'll explain later, but right now you need to eat! I think your dog friend is going to eat it all if you don't."

The dog keeps eyeing the chicken wrapped in tinfoil and the pot of mac and cheese over the fire, trying to figure out a way to get to it without burning himself. I'm pretty sure if we leave him like that he'll figure out a way, too. He looks like a smart dog.

"Yeah," Ethan says. "I'm starved. Sounds good."

11 - Ethan

CHICKEN AND MAC AND CHEESE is just chicken and mac and cheese, but seriously this is amazing. Fuck, I wish there was more. I split the rest of what's left over the fire with my dad, but it doesn't seem like nearly enough. I consider making some more, since I'm sure we've got more somewhere, but it's late.

If I'm being honest, I kind of just want to cuddle the fuck out of Ashley right now. I don't want to waste time making more food. I can do that later, or eat some crackers or something.

Wait. Holy fuck, we've got chips, right? Aw yeah. I sneak away under the guise of offering this weird dog my empty plate so he can lick it clean, but then I grab the bag of chips, too. I go back to the fire, but this time I sit extra close to Ashley. No one's complaining, so I put my arm around her and pull her close to me, too. I take a chip and chomp down on it, then she steals one from me.

Yeah, this is nice.

"So, does anyone want to tell us what happened?" my stepmom asks. "We were worried about you two. We heard howling in the woods earlier."

"Yeah," I say, finishing off another chip. "So..."

I clear my throat and start to tell the story.

"We were in the woods, right? Pretty far, I guess. No clue where we were, but we were being real fucking outdoorsman, manly as fuck, alright? Then I heard something. I turned to my dad, and he just looked at me. It was at that moment that I knew something was wrong, but I couldn't place my finger on it yet. We needed to investigate more. The woods were dark, though. It was like a bad fairytale or something, real fucking ominous."

My dad gives me a weird look, smirking. Ashley and her mom listen intently. Caleb looks doubtful. Yeah, you know what? What the fuck are you even doing here still, dude? I don't know.

Still not sure if I like this Caleb kid. Whatever. He can listen to my story.

"I went in further and then I saw this goofy dog standing there. He was surrounded by this vicious pack of wolves. They were sizing him up or something. I could tell this was serious. It was like a sort of 'join us or we'll eat you' type of deal. So I was like, man, I've got to help this dog. I ran in without thinking and just rushed the wolf pack.

Fur was flying, a whole bunch of shit. Not sure how, but I managed to escape unscathed."

"You fought wolves?" Ashley asks.

"Yeah, damn right, Princess," I say. "That's one of my nicknames, you know? Ethan the Wolf. It's not just for show. I'm the real deal."

"Ethan, no one's ever called you that. You just made it up."

"Hey, how do you know? Do you go to school with me?"

She rolls her eyes at me. Yeah, that's what I thought.

Alright, so no one actually calls me Ethan the Wolf, but it's a cool name, don't you think?

"As I was saying," I continue. "So we save this dog. I was like, Dog, go and be free, but it just kept following me. I understand, since I have that effect on dogs, especially when I save their lives."

Caleb interrupts me. What a fucker. "You've saved more than one dog's life?" he asks, skeptical.

"You going to let me tell this story or what?"

"It does sound like you're exaggerating a little, dear," my stepmom says.

I turn to my dad. He knows what's up. "Help me out here?" I ask him.

"Oh, I'm sure it happened exactly like Ethan's saying," my dad says, trying not to laugh.

"Yeah, see?" I say, nodding. "So, we save this dog, and then we decide to head back. All in a day's work, everything's good, except on our way back, we run into this massive fucking bear. I swear it was thirty feet tall. This is some serious shit right there, and I'm kind of scared, but then I remembered my training. I trained with some of the best back in the day, so I know exactly what to do."

"Back in the day?" Caleb asks. "How old are you even? You're the same age as me."

"Look, kid, don't try and drag me down to your level."

"There's no bear that's thirty feet tall, either," Caleb adds. "That doesn't even exist."

"Fine, whatever. Twenty-five feet. Do I look like I care? I didn't bring a measuring tape with me. Pretty fucking sure the bear wouldn't just stand there and let me measure him, too. Listen, none of this matters. I trained back in the day with some wrestler's from school, and they taught me the bear hug. It's not just some fancy wrestling term, it's shit that lumberjacks use to fight off bears, so I rush the thing and just wrap my arms around it, squeeze hard, and you can tell the bear is like, holy shit what did I get myself into this guy is legit."

"None of the bears around here are even aggressive," Caleb says. "They're more scared of you than you are of them. They run away from people almost as soon as they see them."

I stare at the dog, and the dog stares back at me. You dirty fucking dog... I thought you saved my life? You could have done nothing and the bear would have still run away? Wow. I really thought you were a cool dog, too.

I mean, wait, hold up. I can't believe Caleb is backtalking me. What's up with that? That's more important than the dog, I guess. I'll deal with you later, Dog.

"As I was saying," I say. "The bear ran away, because I'm manly as fuck, and then we got a little lost because it's dark out, but we found our way back."

"Actually, we ended up at a road on the other side of the campground, but we just followed it until we recognized where we were, then came in through the front again."

"Dad?" I say, shaking my head at him. "Are you serious? You're ruining the story."

"None of this even happened, did it?" Ashley asks.

"Some of it happened," I say. "We did find this dog."

"He's kind of cute," she says, smiling and holding her hand out.

"Careful, Princess. This is a trained killer dog, raised by wolves, it's..."

The dog crawls on its belly across the ground towards Ashley's hand, then nuzzles against her foot while she pets him.

"Why do you do this to me, Dog?"

"Can someone tell us the *real* story now?" my stepmom asks.

My dad does, just tells it all. I don't know if it's a good story. No wolves, it was just this dog howling. We did see a bear, but it was probably only four or five feet tall, and it did run away shortly after we saw it...

Seriously, what the fuck, Dog? I thought you saved my life.

And then we found a road and followed it until we found the campground.

He doesn't mention me talking to him about Ashley, though. I guess he doesn't have to. We can talk about that later. Tomorrow or something.

"I'm kind of tired," Ashley says.

"I think we all are," my stepmom says. "Caleb, can you go tell your father that we're all set now? Everyone is back and accounted for."

"Alright. I'll tell him about the dog, too. He'll want to know that. I'll try and find out if anyone's missing a dog. Is it alright if he stays here for tonight?"

I mean, yeah, I guess so? The dog's just making himself comfortable here, lounging by the fire. I reach out and pat his stomach and he rolls side to side, making weird dog noises.

And... yeah, so, that's that. Caleb leaves. The dog stays. We put out the fire. I guess we're going to sleep. My dad and Ashley's mom head into their tent first.

I thought I was going to sleep, but, uh...

Little Miss Perfect slips close to me and stands on tiptoes, whispering into my ear. "I want you inside me," she says.

"Oh yeah?" I ask, one brow raised.

"Mhm..." she murmurs, biting her bottom lip.

Yeah, uh... yeah...

Don't worry. I've got this taken care of.

12 - Ashley

O<small>H MY GOD</small>," I <small>GASP</small>. "E<small>THAN</small>..."

I really don't know how I end up in situations like this, but I'm starting to realize I don't care too much. At least I don't care right now. I'm not sure how long this is going to last. Maybe as soon as we're done I'll change my mind, but for now I'm content being blissfully ignorant of the fact that, um...

Well, we really shouldn't be doing this.

Ethan thrusts hard inside of me. I don't even know when we started having sex. Shortly after I teased and tempted him, I'm sure. I thought it would be fun to tell him that I wanted him, to sound sexy and seductive, and I guess Ethan thought it'd be fun, too.

To be honest, it's turning out to be pretty fun. Who knew?

I open my mouth to moan and beg and plead, forgetting where we are. Ethan remembers, thankfully. He covers my mouth with his hand and turns my head to the side, kissing and sucking my neck.

"Quiet," he says. "I'm pretty fucking sure we shouldn't be doing this right now."

When he lets go of my mouth, I look at him, defiant. "When did that ever stop you?" I ask.

He smirks. "Oh, you want to sass me now, huh?"

I glare at him hard and bite my bottom lip. I can barely see him, but I can see enough. The faint glow of moonlight mixed with the light from the cooling embers of our campfire outside shows me everything I need to see. Ethan kind of looks extra powerful right now, even more dominant, more of a bad boy than usual. The strong lines of his body, his jaw, shoulders, the muscles in his torso... they're all accentuated, looking more defined and sharp, as the dark shadows cover him.

He challenges my body with a harsh thrust, shoving his way forcefully inside of me. I gasp and claw at his back, my nails pressing against his skin. He pushes into me even harder, pulling out, then slamming back in. Our bodies clap together. Oh, I want it. It's shocking, almost too rough, but I love the way his lower abs feel when they slide across my clit as his cock drives deep inside me.

"I thought you said we needed to be quiet?" I hiss at him as he picks up speed, our sexual energy getting louder with each passing second.

Ethan glares at me, but he grins, too. He pushes into me again, but this time he stays there. He grinds and writhes against me, making me squirm and wriggle beneath him. Oh my God, what is he doing? I can feel all of his, his muscles and his strength, his body, his power, and his love...

He's kissing me, almost soft and sweet, except he's deliberately moving so that he's teasing and tormenting my clit. I try to kiss him, I try to remember to kiss him, but mostly my mouth is just open. I can't... oh... oh yes...

"You going to cum or what?" he asks me, grinning deviously. "Come on, Princess... I want to feel it. I want to feel you squeeze around my cock. Come on, baby, give me your orgasm."

"Oh... oh... Ethan... I..."

He starts to move again, but it's different from before. Just up and down, his cock still inside of me, his slick abs sliding from the bottom of my clit to the top. It's like... um... when he eats me out, almost? Devours my pussy, if we're using Ethan terminology. Except this is his entire body doing that, almost like his entire torso is pressed flat against my clit, licking up and down.

Um... it's really good. It's...

I give in to him, I give him my orgasm. My body thrashes beneath his, then tenses, tight. Ethan pulls his hips back, then grinds his cock into me again. I gasp and squeeze and pull at him. My legs wrap around his waist and I try to keep him inside of me, but he just keeps slowly pulling out and then sliding back in. It's... it's really amazing and I can't even begin to describe it, but I want it to keep going forever.

When my climax is calming down, or when I think it's calming down, Ethan starts to flex and twitch inside of me. Oh no...

"You wanted me inside you," he says. "You got it, baby girl. Here you go."

It's so intense and strong. It's different now, because I feel too sensitive, like I can feel every-thing. I close my eyes and picture it. I've seen Ethan when he's cumming before. I've made him cum with my hands and my mouth and I know what it looks like. I can't see it now, but I imagine that exact same thing happening, except inside me. It's so much, so strong, so...

My orgasm returns, clenching and clasping at his cock. I pull him farther into me, clinging to him with my arms and my legs and... and with my pussy. Oh, I want him close to me, all of him, every single part of him. He wraps his hands behind my head and kisses me, my nose, my lips, and then each of my closed eyelids. My eyes flutter open and I see Ethan smiling and looking down at me.

"Is that what you wanted, Princess?" he asks, whispering.

I nod, smiling, shy. "Yes."

It's so perfect, but strange, too. When we're done, I realize exactly what we just did. We're... camping... our parents are in a tent nearby, and there's a dog outside, too. I think I remember hearing the dog scratching at the tent when we first started, but thankfully he gave up later.

We're just out in the middle of the woods, and I'm not sure if this is actually perfect. I'm pretty sure if you asked someone where they wanted to have their most powerfully romantic and provocative experiences, they wouldn't say this. They wouldn't choose our situation, not by a longshot.

I don't know, though. Maybe I wouldn't have chosen it, either, but now that it's happened, I still think it's perfect. Sometimes perfect things happen when you least expect them, and they happen when you don't think they should have ever happened at all.

I guess that's just us, Ethan and I. We don't seem like we fit together, except we fit together perfectly.

He rolls onto his back and I roll with him, nuzzling my cheek against his. I squeeze him tight, half laying on him. He puts his arm around me and looks over at me, smiling.

"Is everything alright?" I ask him.

"Yeah," he says. "We made it back. Got lost in the woods, but whatever. No big deal, right?"

"No, I meant with you and your dad. Did you two talk? He didn't say anything when he saw us, so, um..."

"We talked a little," Ethan says quietly. "We talked about stuff I didn't know I was ever going to talk about, but it was nice. We talked about you, too. About this, and what's going on. We decided to talk about it more tomorrow. I guess all of us talking together is easier. He didn't say anything bad, though. He wasn't mad. I think he was confused and surprised, but I can understand that."

"Maybe we shouldn't have sex again on the camping trip, though," I say. "It's kind of weird, isn't it?"

"Fuck, no," Ethan says. "That's not going to happen."

"What if I say no, though?" I say, making a silly face at him. "You've got to listen to me!"

"Yeah, and you know what? What if I make you beg to say yes? What then? I'm going to have to listen to you, Princess. That's just the way this works."

"Nope, I won't do it. I can be patient."

"Nah, fuck that. I don't even think you can. You know what you said to me before we came in this tent? Yeah, I think we both know."

"I want you inside me," I say, repeating myself from before.

"See? You're already asking for it. What happened to your willpower?"

"I wasn't asking! I was telling you what I said!"

"How am I supposed to know that?" he asks, grinning.

I can feel something under my leg, and, um... it's him. His cock twitches, excited.

I shake my head, fast. "No! Nope! I'm saying no, Ethan!"

He squeezes me and moves as if he's going to roll me onto my back. I'm pretty sure if he does, I'm going to stop saying no really soon, but... nope, he doesn't do it. He laughs at my wide-eyed expression, then kisses me.

"If you want to wait, it's cool," he says. "I get it. Maybe we can just do fun family shit or something."

"Like shower together," I say.

"What the fuck family even does that?" he asks.

"We did it this morning," I point out. "And you're my stepbrother, so..."

"Fuck, you're right," Ethan says, grumbling, defeated.

I giggle and he takes it even further, tickling my sides. I start to laugh, loud. The dog barks outside our tent, alert and excited.

"Can we please go to sleep!" my mom shouts out from her tent. "I need my beauty rest!"

"You're always beautiful, darling," I hear my stepdad say.

"Well, that's true," my mom says, coy. "I'd still like to sleep, though."

"Awww," I say. "Isn't that cute?"

"That's cute?" Ethan asks.

I roll my eyes at him. "Of course it's cute. Your dad said my mom was beautiful no matter what. It's a really nice thing to say."

"Oh."

"You should say that to me," I tell him.

"Nah, my dad already said it to your mom. It loses effectiveness if I say it right after."

I shake my head. "I don't think that's how it works."

"Pretty sure that's how it works," he says, grinning.

"*Ple~ase?*"

Ethan sighs.

"You're always beautiful, Princess."

"You didn't even mean it. You sounded bored. That's boring."

"I love you?" he offers.

"I love you, too, but that's besides the point. Say something nice to me."

"I say nice shit to you all the time."

"Oh yeah, like what?"

We play fight and laugh and whisper and argue quietly until we're too tired and our eyes won't stay open any longer. Ethan holds me close to him. I kiss his cheek softly, muttering something, but I don't even know what I'm saying anymore.

"You really are beautiful," he whispers. "I've always thought you were pretty."

A NOTE FROM MIA

Y<small>AY</small>! Everything looks like it's going to work out...

There's still a little more to go, but everything is coming to a close for this season. I'll finish everything up in the next book, and we'll have some fun scenes to read, too. There's still that hot springs that was mentioned earlier, remember? Definitely don't want to forget that!

I think Ethan made a lot of headway with his dad, though. They don't really talk, but I think they needed to talk, and this was a good way for it to happen. They needed to do it on their own terms in their own way, and I don't think they're very cuddly or huggy type of men, haha. I don't know, it just seemed right for it to happen like this.

Then there's Caleb, who... well, I like Caleb, haha. He's cute, but different. Maybe we'll get to meet Scarlet soon...? Hmmmm...

Also, what's with the dog? There's more about that in the next book, but I think it'll be interesting. Just a little extra.

Some of this will be more important later, though. I'm working on finishing up the Second Season of Stepbrother With Benefits, but I'm also considering a Third Season, so we'll see how that goes. It'll happen if you're interested in it happening, so definitely let me know if you are! You can email me or leave a review or post and send me a message on Facebook if you'd like.

We'll have the end of this season soon, though! And there'll be some fun, also. I think Ashley and Ethan have earned it, don't you? They can finally be themselves and be open about their relationship, at least as far as their parents are concerned.

If you liked this one, I hope you'll leave a review, too! What did you think about Ethan's moment with his dad? Do you think Ashley can keep up her willpower and make this a family friendly vacation, or will it be the sort of *very friendly* type that Ashley's mom mentioned earlier? I'd love to hear what you think!

Bye for now!

~MIA

ABOUT THE AUTHOR

Mia likes to have fun in all aspects of her life. Whether she's out enjoying the beautiful weather or spending time at home reading a book, a smile is never far from her face. She's prone to randomly laughing at nothing in particular except for whatever idea amuses her at any given moment.

Sometimes you just need to enjoy life, right?

She loves to read, dance, and explore outdoors. Chamomile tea and bubble baths are two of her favorite things. Flowers are especially nice, and she could get lost in a garden if it's big enough and no one's around to remind her that there are other things to do.

She lives in New Hampshire, where the weather is beautiful and the autumn colors are amazing.

Manufactured by Amazon.ca
Bolton, ON